Pemb
Tel Fax
pemburylibrary@kent.gov.uk

KT-558-372

2/06

21. JUN 07.

12. 07. JUL

04. OCT 08.

– 5 MAY 2010

1 7 AUG 2010

– 5 MAY 2010

– 7 APR 2011

1 7 APR 2012

2 8 APR 2011

2 6 MAR 2014

2 3 APR 2019

Books should be returned or renewed by the
last date stamped above.

CF

Lingard, Joan
Tilly and the Wild
Goats

CUSTOMER SERVICE EXCELLENCE

For Aedan, Rosa, Shona and Amy. J.L.
For Elin. S.W.

ORCHARD BOOKS
96 Leonard Street, London EC2A 4XD
Orchard Books Australia
32/45-51 Huntley Street, Alexandria, NSW 2015
ISBN 1 84362 420 6 (hardback)
ISBN 1 84362 421 4 (paperback)
First published in Great Britain in HB in 2005
First paperback publication in 2006
Text © Joan Lingard 2005
Illustrations © Sarah Warburton 2005
The rights of Joan Lingard to be identified as the author
and of Sarah Warburton to be identified as the illustrator of this
work have been asserted by them in accordance with the
Copyright, Designs and Patents Act, 1988.
A CIP catalogue record for this book is available
from the British Library.
1 3 5 7 9 10 8 6 4 2 (hardback)
1 3 5 7 9 10 8 6 4 2 (paperback)
Printed in Great Britain

TILLY AND THE WILD GOATS

JOAN LINGARD

Illustrated by Sarah Warburton

ORCHARD BOOKS

CHAPTER 1

"I'm terribly sorry," said Mrs Ewbank in what Tilly called her syrup-sponge voice, "but my nephew needs this cottage. He'll have nowhere to live when he gets back from Australia."

"You mean you're going to chuck us out?" cried Tilly.

"Shush, Tilly," said her mother, who was frowning as if she hadn't quite understood what Mrs Ewbank had said. Her forehead was all crinkled like corrugated paper.

"If you turn us out, we won't have anywhere to live." Tilly glared at Mrs Ewbank.

"I know, I've said I'm sorry, dear. But you must understand that I have to consider my nephew first, with him being family. And he has a young child."

"I'm only nine," said Tilly before her mum could shush her again. "And you can't be very sorry or you wouldn't turn us out at all. We might have to sleep in the woods. I might get pneumonia." A girl in her class had had pneumonia last year, though not from sleeping in the woods.

"Perhaps the council might be able to find you a house," said Mrs Ewbank vaguely.

"They only have six houses in the village," Tilly's mother pointed out.

"And they're all taken."

"You wouldn't have to go immediately, of course. I could let you stay for a month while you look for somewhere."

"A month?" echoed Tilly. "Four weeks?"

"I might be able to stretch it to six but that would be all. Gerald will be back by then. I had hoped to have the place redecorated before he moved in." Mrs Ewbank's eyes swept over their orange and pink walls. Tilly's mother was in a vivid colour phase. She said it warmed your soul. She was inclined to say things like that.

"Would Gerald not like it?" asked Tilly. "It's nice and cheery. Stops you getting down in the dumps. Maybe

Gerald never gets the dumps?"

"I think possibly he would prefer something a little quieter, shall we say?"

Mrs Ewbank heaved herself up from the depths of the sofa. She was rather large and the sofa was rather low. "I must be going," she announced. "I have a lunch engagement."

"I hope she chokes on it" said Tilly after she had gone.

"Now Tilly!"

"Can she do this to us? Turn us out when she wants to?"

"I'm afraid so. I signed a contract

agreeing to one month's notice on either side."

Tilly's mother went into the hall and phoned her best friend, Annabel, who came round straight away to comfort them. She brought with her a banana cake and a pot of marmalade, home made. Every time she brought the jam she said that the colour of the marmalade was a dead ringer for Tilly's hair. She said it now. Tilly

wondered why people had to keep saying the same things. Especially boring things.

At least, though, Annabel hadn't brought her three children, who were all under the age of five and expected Tilly to play with them. If she didn't they yowled non-stop so that in the end she'd give in for the sake of peace. Their father must be at home looking after them.

Tilly's mother put the kettle on for coffee.

"What made you sign that contract, Tanya?" asked Annabel. "You should never have agreed to just one month's notice."

"She wouldn't let me have the place otherwise. I was desperate. We were living in a leaky old caravan and winter was just round the corner."

It had been a horrible caravan, not

like some of the fancy new ones that were as big as bungalows.

"Beggars can't be choosers," chanted Tilly, saying what her mum often said, not that they were actually beggars. Her mum earned money by doing something called reflexology. It meant she massaged people's feet and that helped to make them better. It seemed to work. At least they came back for more.

"Oh well, let's have a piece of banana cake," said Annabel.

They each had a piece of banana cake, Tilly included. One thing about Annabel: she could bake cakes. She baked them for the village tearoom, which earned her what she called 'pin money', though she didn't ever spend it on pins. Tilly's mum said she thought it was called that because long ago men used to give their wives

11

pocket money to buy things like pins to do their sewing. Not many wives did sewing nowadays.

"You know, Tanya, you can always camp with us until you find something," said Annabel. "We won't see you put out on the street."

Camp with Annabel's family? The idea horrified Tilly. In addition to the three yowly children and her husband, who was a big man and took up a lot of space, Annabel had two bad-tempered Siamese cats and a dog. And the house only had two bedrooms. The street sounded better than that!

"Let's put on our thinking caps," said Annabel. "Is there anyone in the neighbourhood who might be moving soon?"

Tilly left them to think and went next door to the cottage tacked onto theirs to consult her friend William. But he was more interested in the picture he was painting than the fact that Mrs Ewbank had given Tilly and her mum notice to go.

"Do you know what I've just said?" demanded Tilly.

"Hang on a minute. I just have to finish this bit before the paint dries."

He was going to put his painting in for a competition. The subject was

'Threatened Species'. Quite a big title. It meant birds or animals that might not survive unless they were looked after. William was doing the capercaille, a bird that was found mostly up in the Highlands. Tilly took a squint.

"Not bad." If the truth be told, though she had no intention of saying it, it was really good. William was the best at art in the whole school. Not that there were that many pupils, not like some of the town ones she'd been to. There were only forty-five children in all and two and a half teachers. It didn't mean that one teacher was cut in half. She just taught for half the week.

"We're going to get chucked out of our house," repeated Tilly. "By the Ewe. What are we going to do?"

William put down his paint brush

and considered for a moment. "Do nothing," he advised. "Don't go."

"You mean refuse?"

"You could just sit there and see what she does."

"Chain ourselves to the floor?" Tilly had heard about people doing things like that.

"If necessary."

"She might get the police and they'd have to come and cut us loose with a saw."

"You'd get in the papers then."

"I don't want to get in the papers!" said Tilly indignantly. "At least not for that. I thought you might have some ideas. After all, you've lived here forever."

William Beattie had been born in this cottage. His granny and grandpa lived in the village, as did his great-granny – who was ninety-eight and still had her wits about her – two aunts and an uncle, and a string of cousins of different ages. Tilly's mother said that nothing got past the Beattie family. If that was the case, they should know about houses that might be coming up for rent.

"We might have to move away," Tilly went on. "Go to Edinburgh or Glasgow. Or Inverness," she added, since that was even further. William had to be made to understand how serious this was. It would be very serious if she and her mum were to be turned out of their home. She liked living here more than anywhere else they'd ever lived. And they'd lived in quite a lot of places. William seemed to think it must be great to keep moving around, but he hadn't tried it.

"I expect we'll think of something," he said. "Let's go and have a look round." He whistled to his dog, who had been sleeping beside the radiator. "Walkies, Sandy." At once Sandy was up on his feet, wagging his tail and heading for the door.

Tilly popped her head round her own door first. "I'm just going along to the village with William. We're going house-hunting."

"The best of luck!" said her mother, a bit sarcastically. "I wish it could be that easy!"

"You might be surprised," said Tilly, as she closed the door behind her.

CHAPTER 2

They took the short cut across the field to the village. A path had been worn down the middle by all the people's feet that had tramped through it. Sandy raced ahead of them, his golden tail swaying from side to side as he cut through the long grass. There were no sheep in the field this morning so William had been able to let him off the lead.

The land belonged to old Mr

Sheridan, who lived alone in the big house. Strictly speaking, it was private, though Mr Barr, the estate manager, turned a blind eye to the locals using it. He wouldn't have been popular if he hadn't, for it took much longer to go round by the road. Even so, he wasn't much liked. He had a temper a bit like Annabel's cats. He snarled easily. One of William's uncles had worked for him for six months and had said that was long enough.

He looked after Mr Sheridan's estate and his wife looked after the house and Mr Sheridan. Mr Sheridan hadn't been seen in the village for years. Some people said he must be ninety, others thought a hundred. And yet some others said he could be dead for all anybody knew. Nobody was ever asked into the house. The postie was kept on the back door step, as was

William's Auntie Netta when she called selling raffle tickets in aid of the village hall fund. It made you wonder, didn't it? Tilly's mother said people talked a lot of nonsense, they could cook things up out of nothing. She liked a gossip herself, though, at times, and she admitted that there did seem to be a bit of a mystery surrounding Mr Sheridan and the big house.

Tilly and William skirted the high stone wall surrounding it.

The door that led into the garden was locked, as usual. They always tried it when they went past, just in case. They couldn't see the downstairs windows because of the wall but the ones upstairs looked blank as if nobody lived inside the rooms. It was rumoured that the attic rooms were haunted by a woman in white who wailed and beat her hands against the walls. William's grandpa said there were probably bats in the roof space.

"Maybe Mr Sheridan would let you rent part of the house," suggested William, not very seriously. "He doesn't need all those rooms."

Tilly didn't think she'd much fancy living inside such a big grey heap of stone, especially if there was a ghost lurking about. It wouldn't be very easy to get to speak to Mr Sheridan anyway.

"Look!" she cried, coming to a halt

and pointing towards the hills. "There go the goats!"

William turned to look.

They loved to see the goats running in a long, thin, brown line, free, the way Sandy did. The goats were wild and they never came close to the village but the villagers were proud of them. They thought of them as their goats. The animals had lived in the glen for hundreds of years.

As they watched, they saw a vehicle coming down the glen, bumping along over the uneven ground. That must be why the goats were running. As the car came closer they realised it was Mr Barr's Range Rover. He was at the wheel, and he had a passenger.

"Who's that with him?" asked Tilly. She counted on William knowing everyone.

He shook his head and called Sandy to heel. The dog came reluctantly and looked fed up when William clipped his lead back onto his collar. William didn't want Sandy to get into a scrap with the manager's bull terrier.

The Range Rover stopped before reaching the field and the two men got out with the bull terrier. The stranger was now setting up a tripod.

"What's he doing?" asked Tilly.

"I think he might be measuring something." One of William's uncles was a surveyor. "My Uncle Tom took me out with him one day when he was measuring up land on a building plot. He had a tripod like that with a kind of measuring thing on top."

"But they're not going to build anything here, are they?"

Mr Barr was taking something out of the back of the car. It looked like a board.

Tilly and William moved on and arrived at the gate at the same time as Mr Barr. The dogs growled at each other and William pulled Sandy back and said, "Sit, Sandy!" Sandy sat reluctantly but kept his eye on the other dog, who was not on a leash.

"What are you kids doing snooping about?" demanded Mr Barr.

"We're not snooping," said Tilly, eyeing the board he was holding. "We're just going to the village. We're house-hunting."

"Go do your house-hunting somewhere else! You're trespassing."

"We always come this way," said William.

"Not any more." The manager

26

showed them the front of the board.

STRICTLY PRIVATE, it said. KEEP OUT.

"What's that for?" asked Tilly.

"Can't you read?" Mr Barr opened the gate. "Out you go, and I don't want to see you in here again. I'm sick of people traipsing around making nuisances of themselves, dropping litter."

"We don't drop litter," objected Tilly.

At that moment the bull terrier made a rush for Sandy and Sandy leapt up tugging at his lead, desperate to get at him, though he was not normally a fighting dog. But if he was being attacked he wouldn't sit still. Both dogs growled and snarled and danced around each other. The manager grabbed at the bull terrier's collar and hauled him off.

"You shouldn't be bringing a dog in here," he said. "Look at the trouble you're causing! Out!"

They went.

He closed the gate behind them, slid the bolt into position, took a padlock out of his bag and snapped it into place. Tilly and William watched while he did it.

"What are you waiting for?" he demanded.

"We were wondering what that man was doing?" said Tilly.

Mr Barr turned his head briefly to look at him. "It's none of your business so why don't you just scram? Talk about nosy kids! What's your name, anyway?"

"Tilly. Tilly Trotwood."

"Well, Tilly Trotwood, I don't want to see you on Mr Sheridan's property again. I'm warning you! You, too, William Beattie."

"If you ask me," said Tilly as they walked away, "he's up to no good."

The first house in the village was Mrs Ewbank's. It was set back from the road behind a walled garden and was the biggest in the district, leaving aside Mr Sheridan's.

"I don't see why her nephew couldn't stay there with her," said Tilly.

"Annabel says she's got six bedrooms."

"I don't think she will, though," said William, "let her nephew stay."

Tilly sighed.

The rest of the houses in the village were one and two-storey cottages, and all of them were occupied. At the far end were the six houses owned by the council, also full.

"I think the best plan," said William, "would be to put up a notice in the shop."

The notice board in the shop was always covered with postcards advertising things for sale from bicycles to bridesmaids' dresses (worn only once). There were also wanted ads.

The shop was empty except for Mrs Paterson behind the counter. She greeted them cheerfully.

"What can I do for you two today?"

"Mrs Ewbank's going to turn my mum and me out of our house," announced Tilly.

"Oh dear." Mrs Paterson's smile dropped away. "I am sorry."

"She needs it for her nephew."

"Oh, is Gerald coming back?"

"Yes, he is. I don't suppose you'd know of anything coming up?"

"I'm afraid not, dear."

"We thought we might be able to put up a notice on the board?" said William.

"Of course." Mrs Paterson gave them a postcard and said nothing about paying for it, which was just as well since they didn't have any money on them. She also lent them a pen.

"What shall I say?" Tilly bit the end of the pen, forgetting that it wasn't hers. "Homeless." She printed it out.

"You're not homeless yet," William pointed out.

"We soon will be." In brackets behind it Tilly wrote (soon to be) in small letters. "And nowhere to go. Please help! That should do, shouldn't it?" At the foot she put her mother's name and her own and their address.

The postcard then looked like this:

"Better put your phone number too," said William.

Tilly added that and by then there wasn't much room left on the card. But there was a space along the top.

"Would you have a red pen I could borrow?" she asked Mrs Paterson.

The shopkeeper took a new one

from the stand. "You can have a loan of this for a minute."

Tilly printed **URGENT** in big red letters along the top, then she held the card up for inspection.

"Do you not think you should let your mum see it first?" said Mrs Paterson. "I don't know that I should put it up till she does."

"It'll be all right, really it will. There's no time to waste. And Mum's busy this afternoon. She's got three lots of feet to do."

"Oh well, if you're sure." Mrs Paterson didn't sound too sure herself.

"Her mum won't mind," said William. "I expect she'd write it just like that herself."

Mrs Paterson gave Tilly a drawing pin.

While Tilly was pinning the card onto the board, the door pinged open and in came William's Auntie Netta, known to be the one of biggest gossips in the village. She was wearing her pink furry slippers so she must have come out in a hurry.

"I've just had Muriel Mackie on the phone," she announced, almost out of breath. Mrs Mackie was another gossip and her husband, being the postie, was able to bring home a lot of news. "She heard they're going to build a golf course in the glen."

"I can't believe that," said Mrs Paterson.

"I can," said Tilly. "There was a man out there measuring it up."

"And Muriel says," said Auntie Netta, pausing for another breath, "that means they'll have to get rid of the goats!"

CHAPTER 3

The village was in an uproar. The news spread like a forest fire on a hot summer's day. William's Auntie Netta must have rapped on a few doors on her way along for, within minutes, the shop was full of people all talking at once.

"Get rid of our goats so that folk can knock a wee white ball about!"

"What a nerve."

"A golf course of all things!"

"Mr Sheridan would never sell the land."

But when everyone calmed down Mrs Paterson pointed out that no one knew what Mr Sheridan would do since he hadn't been seen in years. Then the minister, who had also come in, said that he thought it was very unlikely anyone would get planning permission to change the use of the land.

"Let's not get too worked up about it until we know some hard facts," he cautioned. "It might all just be a rumour."

There was a murmur of agreement.

"Except that there was a man along there up to something," muttered Tilly darkly. "With Mr Barr."

By this time the crowd was dispersing. Nobody had had time to read Tilly's postcard. They'd been too busy talking to each other.

Tilly and William left the shop when everyone else had gone. Sandy bounded down the step, straining at his lead. He'd had enough of people's legs jostling him. Somebody had stepped on the end of his tail. They hadn't even heard him yelp, they'd been so busy talking.

Outside on the pavement, Auntie Netta was chatting to William's Auntie Jean, who had come along to the shop for a pint of a milk. Auntie Netta was bringing Auntie Jean up to date with the news.

"You know, Auntie Netta, I think you're right," said Tilly. She called her 'auntie' even though she wasn't a real aunt to her. She did the same with all William's aunts and uncles. She'd been told to. Her only real aunt and uncle lived in Yorkshire.

"I'll keep my ear to the ground," promised Auntie Netta, "and I'll let you know if I hear anything else."

Tilly and William carried on to the end of the street. Sandy was desperate to get into the field but he was in for a disappointment. He barked hopefully but the gate was still firmly padlocked. The board saying STRICTLY PRIVATE, KEEP OUT had been erected at the side of it. There was no sign of either the estate manager or the surveyor.

Tilly and William leant on the gate and gazed across the field. They could see their houses from here. They were only five to ten minutes walk away, if you went by the path through the field.

They could, of course, climb the fence but that didn't seem like a good idea. If they did, it would be just their luck to walk smack into Mr Barr and his nasty dog. The road, it would have to be.

"Look," cried Tilly excitedly. "Do you see a face? Up there, at one of the top windows in the big house."

William looked and he did see a face, but it was too far away to make out anything much about it.

"I think it's Mr Sheridan," said Tilly.

"Could be," agreed William.

The next minute the face had disappeared.

It took them a good twenty minutes to walk home by the road and Sandy had to stay on the lead, which didn't please him one little bit. He let them know by dragging on his lead. There was no footpath so every time they heard a car coming they had to stop and stand in to the side.

Once, when they looked round, they saw, rounding the corner, the small blue van that belonged to William's father. He was a plumber and he worked in a town ten miles away. He drew up beside them.

"What are you two up to then?"

Why did everyone always think they were up to something? Usually they were minding their own business. Well, more or less.

Tilly told Mr Beattie about the rumour.

He frowned. "As a matter of fact, there could be some truth in it. I heard something in town this morning. They say they might get planning permission since it's scrubland. Nothing grows there, except heather. They think a golf course would bring tourists into the area."

41

"Tourists," sniffed Tilly.

"We need them. They give people work and there aren't many jobs around."

 But the goats!" cried Tilly.

"They wouldn't put them down. They'd move them somewhere else."

"We don't want them moved," said William. "This is their home."

"Oh well, I don't suppose we can do much about it. Do you want a lift?'

But it wasn't worth getting into the back of the van, which was full of tools, anyway. They said they'd walk. Mr Beattie drove on.

"Why do grown-ups always say there's not much they can do about it?" said Tilly. "We'll have to do something about it, you and me. If nobody else is going to."

"What can we do?"

"Start a petition. That's what all the mothers did in the last place we lived. They wanted speed bumps on the road to stop cars going so fast and running children down."

"Did it work?"

"It did. We got the bumps."

"I'll come round after tea then. We'll draw one up."

Tilly's mum gave them a hand, once she'd done her last pair of feet.

She said they should set the petition up on the computer, rather than print it out by hand. It would look more professional.

This is what they wrote:

"The wild goats have lived on these hills for hundreds of years. They are unique and should be preserved in their own habitat. We strongly object to the idea of them being evicted to make way for a golf course."

After they had run the spell check to make sure they'd made no mistakes, they printed it out. They printed a dozen copies until Tilly's mother said she thought that would do.

Tilly was first to sign the petition, followed by William, and then Tilly's mum.

"It's a start," said Tilly, gazing at the page, which now read below:

Tilly Trotwood, 4 Bank Cottages
William Beattie, 3 Bank Cottages
Tanya Trotwood, 4 Bank Cottages

They then went next door to William's house and both his parents signed. So did his sister Mandy, who was seven but could write her name clearly in joined-up writing. His older brother John, who was fifteen, was not in.

Old Mrs Black lived at number two. She had a problem with her hearing.

"Goats?" she cried. "What goats?"

"On the hills," shouted Tilly. "Out there!"

"I don't know any goats."

"She won't understand," said William.

Tilly gave up with reluctance since every single signature was precious. They carried on along to number one. Mr and Mrs Sharp did B&B in the summer season.

"What's it all about then?" asked Mr Sharp, putting on his glasses and

taking the piece of paper into his hand.

William explained.

"A golf course eh? That could be good for bringing in visitors."

"Americans especially," said Mrs Sharp. "They like coming to Scotland to play golf."

"There are lots of golf courses in Scotland already," put in Tilly anxiously. She had a horrible feeling they weren't going to sign.

"It could be good for business," said Mr Sharp to his wife.

They didn't sign.

"People are more important than goats," said Mr Sharp, handing back the petition.

"We're not saying they aren't," countered Tilly. "But they could put a golf course somewhere else."

Mr and Mrs Sharp were not going

to change their minds so Tilly and William left.

"It's not going to be as easy as we thought," said William.

CHAPTER 4

They had more luck in the village the next day. They went from house to house and managed to get signatures from all the people who had been in the shop the day before. But Mrs Paterson, the shopkeeper, didn't sign.

"I'm sorry to disappoint you," she said, "but I have to be honest with you. I would welcome more trade."

Tilly and William were taken aback.

"I thought you liked the goats," said Tilly.

"I've got nothing against them but I have to think of my own livelihood. It's not easy making a living in a small shop these days."

"My mum and I buy nearly everything from you," said Tilly.

"That's because you haven't got a car," said Mrs Paterson. "But the folk that do, go to the supermarket in the town for a lot of their stuff."

Mr Busby, who owned the pub, the Black Bull, didn't sign either. "Sorry, kids. The more thirsty customers, the better, as far as I'm concerned."

But Jessie, who owned the cafe, did put her name down, even though the golf course might have brought her in a few extra customers for tea and scones. She kept a copy of the petition on the counter and invited customers to sign

it, even those who didn't live in the district. They had a right to an opinion too, she said, since they came to enjoy the peace and quiet of the countryside.

The postie and his wife signed, as did Mr Flynn, the school janitor, and his wife. Mrs Graham, the head teacher, was away on holiday with her family, but Mr Flynn said he was sure she'd be on for the petition when she returned.

All of William's relatives signed,

down to the age of five and up to ninety-three. His great-granny was highly indignant. She had known the goats since she was a child and since she was the oldest person in the village, she had known them the longest. The Beattie family took up a whole page on their own and part of another one.

Tilly and William cycled to all the houses in the outlying area, determined to go to each and every one.

Sandy didn't like it when they went out on their bikes because he had to be left behind. They couldn't have him running along the road behind them. It would be too dangerous. When Sandy saw William putting on his helmet, his tail drooped. With the field being out of bounds now, the only place a dog could have a decent run was in the wood and the children weren't allowed to go into the wood without an adult.

It took a few days to get round everybody. Sometimes the people were out, so they'd have to go back again. But gradually the sheets filled up. And the important thing was that more people were against the golf course than for it. They had over 300 signatures.

"That's fantastic." Tilly's mother was impressed.

"I don't suppose I could get up a

petition asking Mrs Ewbank not to put us out?" said Tilly.

"No, you could not."

"Everyone's saying it's a shame."

"That's different from signing a petition."

So far, Tilly's postcard on the shop noticeboard had not brought in any offers. Her mother thought they might have to start looking in the town. Tilly hated that idea.

"And don't tell me beggars can't be choosers," she said.

The one person Tilly and William had not visited was Mrs Ewbank. William thought they should ask her. They might offend her if they didn't.

"I don't care if we offend her. She's offended us!"

"I still think we should ask her," said William stubbornly.

"She won't sign," predicted Tilly.

"I'll do it if you don't want to come."

Tilly said he could do the asking but she would come with him. She had never been inside Mrs Ewbank's house and she might just ask them in. Tilly was not going to pass up the opportunity.

On their way along to the village, they met Auntie Netta, who had another piece of news. She'd heard there was to be a hotel beside the course, as well as a clubhouse, and maybe even some houses.

"Before we know it they'll be building a whole town!" she said.

"I don't think Mrs Ewbank would

fancy the village being turned into a town," said Tilly.

When they reached her gate William undid the latch and walked up the drive first. He rang the bell.

After a moment Mrs Ewbank opened the door. "Yes?" She didn't sound too friendly.

William cleared his throat and started to explain about the goats. She'd heard, she said. They had better come in. She took them into her sitting room and asked them to sit down. Tilly had a good look around. Little china ornaments rested on every ledge. Some were shepherds and shepherdesses, others were animals. Rabbits, squirrels, horses, cats and dogs. On a white fluffy rug in front of the fireplace lay three Siamese cats. It was just as well they hadn't brought Sandy!

"It's absolutely frightful," said Mrs Ewbank.

They weren't sure whether she meant the petition or the goats being evicted so they kept quiet.

"Those poor goats," Mrs Ewbank went on. "The very idea of turning them out of their habitat is disgraceful."

"You'll sign the petition then?" said Tilly, who had resolved beforehand to keep her mouth shut.

"I most certainly will."

57

Mrs Ewbank's glasses hung from a gold chain round her neck. She brought them up to her eyes to examine the wording on the form. She nodded approvingly and then signed her name with a flourish. Antoinette Ewbank. Tilly couldn't imagine anyone calling the Ewe 'Antoinette'.

"You should be congratulated for doing this," she said, as she handed the paper back. "A worthy cause."

She rewarded them with a lump of Turkish Delight each and wished them the best of luck.

"She's not such a bad old stick," said William, as they walked off, chewing their sweets. Neither of them was very fond of Turkish Delight but they ate it, anyway.

58

"Except that she's putting my mum and me out," Tilly reminded him.

"She can't help it, though, can she? Not if her nephew needs the house."

"Don't you start taking her side, William Beattie!" Tilly tossed her head, annoyed with him.

"You've got to see it from her point of view too, haven't you?"

"No, I have not," retorted Tilly hotly. "You don't care, do you, if my mum and me have to sleep in the woods? It's all right for you, nobody's going to take your house away."

She marched on ahead of him and went into her own house and slammed the door behind her.

"What's up with you?" asked her mother.

"I don't want to play with William any more."

Her mother smiled.

"I don't."

After tea William came in.

"What do you want?" demanded Tilly.

"Still on your high horse?"

She glared at him.

"I was just thinking about the petition. We've got all these names but what are we going to do with them?"

"How do you mean?" asked Tilly.

"Well, we've got to give it to somebody, haven't we?"

"What about the council offices?" suggested Tilly's mother.

"My dad says no one knows if Mr Sheridan has sold the land yet. He thinks the golf people will be seeing if

they can get planning permission
before they buy."

"Makes sense," said Tilly's mother.

"That means..." said Tilly slowly.

"That we should give the petition to Mr Sheridan," finished William.

CHAPTER 5

The problem now was how to get the petition to Mr Sheridan.

"You could ask Mr Barr to deliver it." To Tilly's mum that seemed the obvious solution, but she didn't know him as well as they did.

"No!" trumpeted Tilly and William together.

"No?"

"He might not do it," said Tilly. "Even if he said he would."

"You don't trust him?"

"No!" Again, they spoke simultaneously.

"We think he wants the golf course," explained William.

"He was with the man doing the measuring," added Tilly.

"What about asking the postie then?"

That seemed a better idea. They went to see Mr Mackie when he'd finished his rounds.

He was quite willing to take the petition. "But I always hand the letters over to Mrs Barr. I never see Mr Sheridan."

"In that case," said William, "we'll just have to think of some other way."

"The only way," declared Tilly, as they walked back home, "is to take it ourselves."

"Easier said than done!"

Tilly agreed. If they were to go up to house and knock on the door it would be Mrs Barr who would answer it.

For a few days they didn't know what to do.

William had to go and visit some other cousins in Edinburgh with his mother one day, which meant that Tilly was on her own. Two of her other school friends, Lindsey and Kathryn, were away on holiday.

"They've gone to Disneyland," she moaned. "Lucky them!"

"Why don't you find something to do?" said her mum. "Have you nothing to read?"

"I've finished my library books."

The village was too small to have its own library. A van did come round but it didn't have space for as many books as Tilly would have liked. She was a fast reader. Too fast, in the opinion of her mother, who got fed up when she read the last line of a book, closed it, and immediately complained, "I've got nothing to read."

"There must be something you can do. Why not paint a picture? Like William's been doing for that competition."

"William's good at drawing and painting. He's done a brilliant picture of a capercaille." He had already sent it in.

"You could try."

Tilly went up to her bedroom. For want of anything better to do she got out her paints and paintbrush. She had not used either of them very much.

She'd always thought she wasn't much good at art. But now she was thinking about the competition 'Endangered Species.' Their goats were endangered. If they were moved they might not survive. They might be miserable in a new place. She filled an old jam jar with water from the bathroom.

She was going to paint the goats. She couldn't do them in the way that William had done his capercaille, painting in every detail. But perhaps she could do a picture of the goats running free, in a long, thin, brown line through the hills.

She went across the landing to her mother's room and borrowed her binoculars. She put them to her eyes. The goats were there, not running, but grazing peacefully. But she could still see them running in her mind's eye.

For the next couple of hours she was taken up by the goats. While she was painting she forgot about everything else.

When she went downstairs her mum asked her, "So what have you been doing?"

"Painting a picture, like you said." But Tilly didn't say what she had been painting. She wanted to keep it a secret at the moment. And it might not be any good. It was probably too late to put it into the competition anyway.

The following morning, William came round to call for her again. They took Sandy along the road to the village. William had to collect some groceries for his mother and Tilly had to buy a newspaper for hers so that they could look at properties to let. When they opened the door of the shop they were surprised to see Mrs Barr at the counter. It wasn't often that she was seen in the village. She usually phoned in her orders to the shop and her husband picked them up.

She was wearing a pale pink suit, with a flower in the button hole, and spiky, high-heeled shoes, and she was talking to Mrs Paterson.

"It's Mr Barr's niece. She's marrying a bank manager." Mrs Barr seemed to be very pleased about that. "The wedding's in Edinburgh."

Tilly and William looked at each other.

"Nice day for a wedding," commented Mrs Paterson.

A horn tooted outside.

"That'll be Bert," said Mrs Barr. "How much do I owe you?"

"Ten fifty."

Mrs Barr paid and Mrs Paterson passed a bag over the counter. The horn tooted again outside.

"Have a good day," said Mrs Paterson.

Mrs Barr clattered out on the high heels that seemed a little too high for her. She had to go carefully down the step, putting a hand on the wall to steady herself. Tilly and William watched as she got into the Range Rover and the Barrs drove off to the wedding in Edinburgh. They turned again to look at each other. So the Barrs were off to Edinburgh. And the chances were that they would be away for the whole day.

William collected his mother's groceries and Tilly bought a

71

newspaper and then they took their shopping home. Since Mr Barr was on his way to Edinburgh they decided to take the short cut across the field.

It would save time. They climbed the gate and Sandy crawled between the bars. William unhooked his lead and he raced up and down, over the moon at being set free.

When they reached the road on the other side the dog was less happy and had to be coaxed to come to heel. But William and Tilly could not afford to waste any more time. They had important business to attend to. And they could not take Sandy with them.

Tilly fetched the petition from her

house and, at the last minute, decided to borrow her mother's mobile phone. She tucked it into her pocket, saying nothing about it, or where she was going, to her mother.

"The phone was a good idea," said William, as they set off along the road, in the opposite direction to the village.

The gate to the big house was only a few minutes' walk from their cottages. At the entrance stood the stone lodge where the Barrs lived. No one would be at home today, except for the bull terrier. He came to the window as they went by and barked furiously, his nostrils flaring. Tilly made a face at him, since he was safe behind glass.

The drive wound its way between tall rhododendron bushes. They were past their flowering time, though a few pink and purple blossoms still clung to the branches. Finally, the house came into view.

They slowed their steps a little. It did look rather off-putting, being so big and so high, with all those windows and not a sign of life at any of them. They went round to the back door and William tried the handle. Locked. Should they ring the bell?

"I don't suppose Mr Sheridan will come and answer it," said William.

Tilly tried, anyway. Nothing happened.

"He might not have heard it," said William. "It probably only rings at the back of the house, where the kitchen is."

"We'd better try the front door then," said Tilly.

They went round to the front and climbed the seven steep steps leading up to the heavy door.

"It looks as if no one's opened it for years," said William.

The brass knocker was the shape of a lion's head. Tilly took a firm grip of it and knocked several times. They listened. They lifted the letter-box flap and tried to peer through the slot but found themselves looking into darkness.

"I think he's dead," said Tilly.

"If he is, how can he sell the land?" asked William.

He knocked this time. Again, nobody came.

They went back down the steps and onto the lawn to get a better view of the house.

"Look!" cried Tilly. "There's a face at that window." She pointed. "Do you see? On the first floor?"

William did see.

"It's a man," said Tilly. "An old man. It must be Mr Sheridan." She waved.

CHAPTER 6

The old man pushed up the window and stuck his head out. He had wispy white hair and brown spots on his forehead. He looked really old.

"Hello," he called down. His voice was wavery and they could only just make out what he was saying.

"Hello," Tilly called back up. "Are you Mr Sheridan?"

"I am."

"We've come to see you."

"To see me?"

"Yes, to see you."

The man scratched his head.

Well, of course, nobody ever did go to see him so he must be surprised.

"Who are you?"

"Tilly Trotwood and William Beattie."

"Should I know you?"

"We live along the road in Bank Cottages."

"Bank Cottages?"

William felt they could go on like this for a long time so he shouted up as politely as he could, "Do you think we could come in and see you?"

"Come in? Oh, I don't know about that."

"It's about something important," said William.

"We're not going to mug you or anything like that," promised Tilly.

"How do I know? You read things in the papers."

"We've come about the goats," said Tilly.

"The goats? You mean the wild goats in the hills?"

"They want to build a golf course there," said William.

"And get rid of the goats," added Tilly.

Mr Sheridan said nothing now. He was frowning and staring out towards the hills. Perhaps he could see the goats though they weren't sure about that. His eyesight would probably not be good enough.

"I think we've confused him," said William in a quiet voice. "My great-gran gets muddled at times. Other times she's O.K. He must be about the same age as her."

"What are we going to do?" said Tilly. "We can't stand here shouting out everything about the petition and Mr Barr and the man measuring the land and all of that. Somebody might hear us if they came over the field. We don't want to attract attention."

They certainly did not. Tilly knew her mother would be furious if she could see her. And if she knew she was planning to go inside this strange house she would have a fit. But Tilly was sure this old man was safe enough. They wouldn't think of going in if the Barrs were around.

She tilted her head back again to look at Mr Sheridan. "You really would be quite safe with us."

Mr Sheridan still did not look

convinced. "Mr Barr always says not to let anybody in. The village is full of thieves."

"Mr Barr's a liar," Tilly informed him.

Mr Sheridan stared down at her. "You should watch what you say, young lady."

"It's true," said William.

"Thieves broke in and stole my silver," Mr Sheridan said pointedly.

"When was that?" asked William.

"Not long ago."

They hadn't heard anything about a break in at the big house in the village.

"We think Mr Barr is trying to sell your land to some people for a golf course," said Tilly.

"He can't do that. He'd need my signature." Mr Sheridan frowned, as if he was thinking about something.

"Well, I don't really know," he went on less certainly.

"Maybe we could come in and talk to you?" suggested Tilly. "We've show you, signed by all the people in the village. Well, nearly all."

They could see he was wavering. They waited, holding their breath. He must let them in. They didn't know when they'd get such a good chance again, with the Barrs being away in Edinburgh. It wouldn't be every week that they'd be off to a wedding.

"Trouble is," said Mr Sheridan, "I can't come down the stairs to open the door. I'm in a wheelchair, you see."

That was a blow.

"But you could see if any of the windows would open," Mr Sheridan said.

"Would that be all right?" asked William.

"I can give you permission. It's my house."

"Let's go!" cried Tilly.

They did a tour of the outside, checking every window. Each one was securely locked.

"No go," reported William on their return.

"Oh, dear," said Mr Sheridan.

"You wouldn't have a key you could throw down?" asked Tilly.

"I'm afraid not. Mrs Barr keeps them in a cupboard downstairs." Mr Sheridan pushed his head a bit further out of the window and looked down at the wall below. Then he said to William, "There's a drain pipe there, lad."

"I could climb it," said William eagerly.

"I wouldn't want you to break your neck though. Dear me, no, that would be dreadful."

"I wouldn't, I promise."

"William is brilliant at climbing trees," put in Tilly. "He rescued the minister's cat from the top of an oak tree."

"Very well, then. The pipe leads up to the bathroom so I shall go there and open the window for you, William. Wait till I do it."

It seemed to take ages before Mr Sheridan's head appeared at the bathroom window. They had been beginning to get jumpy. But they'd realised he would have to manoeuvre his wheelchair round all the awkward corners in the house and then wrestle with the window to get it up. Now finally he'd made it.

"All right, lad."

William put his right foot up as high as he could onto the pipe, then he began to haul himself upwards. In no time at all he had reached the bathroom window sill and was clambering in. His head poked out now.

"I'll go and let you in at the front door," he called down to Tilly.

Tilly waited excitedly on the top step. She heard footsteps, a key turning, bolts rattling, and then the big heavy door creaked open.

"Enter!" said William.

Tilly stepped into the dark hall and William locked and bolted the door behind them.

CHAPTER 7

Gradually, Tilly's eyes adjusted to the dim light. Facing them was a wide staircase with gold-framed pictures climbing up the walls on either side. They were dark paintings, and all of people from long ago. They were probably Mr Sheridan's ancestors.

At the top of the stairs sat Mr Sheridan himself in his wheelchair.

"Welcome to Sheridan Hall! Please do come up." He had a very polite voice.

Tilly and William mounted the stairs, taking their time. They felt running up them might not be the right thing to do.

When they reached Mr Sheridan, he held out his hand to Tilly and said, "I'm very pleased to meet you, Tilly." His hand felt cool and papery. She didn't say anything. She felt a bit tongue-tied, which was not usual for her.

"Please," Mr Sheridan continued, "come with me."

He went ahead of them in his chair, down a long corridor, and then turned into a room furnished with two sofas, several large chairs and a big desk at the window. It was an old-fashioned room and the chintz covers on the sofas and chairs were faded. Once, the roses on them would have bloomed brightly, but not now.

"Do have a seat."

Tilly and William sat down, side by side, on one of the sofas. They felt themselves sinking into it and as they did, a puff of dust arose.

Mrs Barr couldn't be that good a

housekeeper. Mr Sheridan's eyes wouldn't be sharp enough to notice a bit of dust here and there.

"Now tell me what is all this about the goats?"

"There's a plan to move them out of the hills and turn the land into a golf course," said William.

"But the land belongs to me." Mr Sheridan frowned. "At least I'm sure it does."

"It does," stressed Tilly. "Unless you've sold it to somebody else."

"Why would I do that?"

"For money?"

"What do I want with more money at my age? I have as much as I need."

"Mr Barr seems to think you're selling the land," said William.

"Do you mean my estate manager?" Mr Sheridan was looking even more puzzled.

"He was with a man who was measuring up the land." Tilly spoke urgently. She must make him understand how serious all this was. "A surveyor. We saw him with our own eyes."

"This is all very curious. I must have a word with Mr Barr."

"I don't think that would be a good idea," said Tilly.

"Really? Why not? Mr Barr looks after my affairs for me."

Tilly and William were silent for a moment. They wished they could discuss it and decide what to tell Mr Sheridan, but it would be rude to whisper to each other in front of him. This was tricky. Could they tell him that they thought his manager was trying to cheat him?

"I must have a word with Mrs Barr." Mr Sheridan reached out and pressed a bell in the wall.

"Mrs Barr's not here," said Tilly. "They've gone to a wedding in Edinburgh."

"So they have. I'd quite forgotten. Mr Sheridan looked thoughtful. "She's left me a cold meal in the next room. I have all my rooms up the stairs now. So much better, all on one level."

He began to tell them how he'd had all the rooms upstairs adapted for his chair. For a while he seemed to forget about the goats and the golf course. They had to bring him back to the subject.

"So you don't want to sell your land?" asked William.

"My land? Certainly not!'

"Or put the goats out?"

"Indeed no. I have always been fond of the goats."

"We have a petition here," said Tilly, "signed by more than 300 people, all of them objecting to the goats being evicted."

"300 people? My goodness."

"Would you like to see it?" Tilly held the sheets of paper out to him.

"I would very much, except I wouldn't be able to read it. My glasses broke a couple of weeks ago, you see, and Mr Barr had to take them to an optician to get them mended."

"Has it taken two weeks?" William smelt a rat. When his grandpa had broken his glasses the optician had mended them the next day.

"Might be more," said Mr Sheridan vaguely. "Such a nuisance, being without them. I can't even read the paper."

"Mr Sheridan," said William, "have you signed any papers recently?"

"Please think," urged Tilly.

"Let me see. There was one about council tax or something like that. I don't know what half of these things are. Mr Barr is very good. He understands everything. Saves me the bother."

"Did you see 'council tax' written on the paper?" asked William.

"Oh no, how could I? My glasses were broken. Mr Barr told me where to sign. He had a friend with him who countersigned. A lawyer from Edinburgh. Or maybe it was Glasgow, I don't quite recall. Nice enough fellow."

Tilly and William exchanged sidelong glances. The paper would be nowhere in the house now, that was for sure. How were they to convince Mr Sheridan that his estate manager was not to be trusted? They had no proof, except what they had told him already.

"Do you have any children?" asked Tilly. If he did it would be easier to talk to them.

"Children? I'm afraid not. I never married."

"Or any other relations?'

"I have a second cousin in Australia. Haven't seen him in years. Cedric will get this place when I go, if he outlives me, that is. Otherwise his son will inherit. It will stay in the hands of the family at any rate."

"You've left it in your Will?" asked Tilly.

"Oh yes. All signed and sealed. Everything will go to Cedric except for a few bequests. I thought Mr and Mrs Barr should be rewarded for their service to me."

Tilly and William groaned. Goodness knows how much the Barrs were going to get in the Will! They themselves were getting nowhere and time was moving on. Their mothers would soon start wondering where they were. Tilly thought about phoning her mother on the mobile but she'd have to tell her they were here. And then her mother would come steaming along the road at the double.

"We think," began William, deciding to come straight out with it, "that Mr Barr is trying to cheat you, Mr Sheridan. We think that when you signed that form you might have sold your land."

"That is a very serious statement, young man." Mr Sheridan looked at

William severely. "I cannot believe Mr Barr would deceive me in this way. That form I signed had to do with income tax."

"You said council tax before," said Tilly.

"Whatever. I get a bit muddled at times."

"You're telling me!" thought Tilly.

"Can you substantiate your claim?" asked Mr Sheridan.

"You mean prove it?" asked Tilly.

"I do."

They had nothing to say.

"One really should not make allegations without proof," said Mr Sheridan. "I have complete confidence in Mr and Mrs Barr. They have served me for many years."

"We'd better be going," muttered William.

They stood up.

"You must come back and visit me

another day," said Mr Sheridan. "I shall ask Mrs Barr to invite you for tea. She makes excellent sponge cakes. Very light, with jam in the middle. Where was it you said you lived?"

"Bank Cottages," answered Tilly, knowing that Mrs Barr would never invite them. Especially if Mr Sheridan were to tell her what they'd said. But he might not even remember.

They were about to make for the door when they heard a noise downstairs. They froze. It couldn't possibly be the Barrs, could it? They were – they should be – in Edinburgh.

CHAPTER 8

The Barrs had gone halfway to Edinburgh when their Range Rover had broken down. The gasket had blown. They'd had to phone a garage and they'd sent someone to tow them back to the town, the town ten miles away from their home. It was out of the question then to go to the wedding in Edinburgh, even though the garage was lending them a car. They'd be far too late. Mrs Barr was furious with Mr Barr

99

even though it hadn't been his fault, or not entirely. She'd spent all that money on a new outfit and now had nowhere to wear it!

She was still annoyed with him when they arrived back at Sheridan Hall. "I told you I heard a funny noise in the engine more than a week ago. You should have done something about it."

"I've been too busy."

"Running around with that golf man!"

"You shouldn't grumble about that. It means dough in our pockets. A lot of dough. We'll be able to get out of here."

William stood on the upstairs landing listening, petrified. What a pity Mr Sheridan's hearing wasn't better than it was. Then he would have heard what Mr Barr had said about money in their pockets.

William had no idea how they were
going to get out of this mess. His heart
was thudding. Bump, bump, bump. He
could feel it. Any minute now the
Barrs might come up the stairs to see
Mr Sheridan. And find him! He was
afraid to move even a foot in case a
floorboard creaked. Tilly had remained
in the doorway of Mr Sheridan's room,
her eyes wide open, like saucers.

The Barrs were still arguing below, making quite a racket. William risked a whisper.

"Phone," he said.

Tilly nodded, tiptoed back inside the room and closed the door as gently as she could. She put her back to it and took the mobile phone out of her pocket.

"What are you doing, young lady?" asked Mr Sheridan.

"I have to make a phone call." Tilly dialled, her fingers fumbling over the numbers so that she had to do it twice. "Hello. Mum? It's me, Tilly," she gabbled as fast as she could. "Listen, we need help. William and me are in the big house. Yes,

102

Sheridan Hall. And the Barrs have just come back. Help, quickly, please!"

The Barrs had heard the door closing, even though Tilly had tried to do it gently. They came straight up the stairs and saw William standing on the landing.

Mr Barr seized him. "What are you doing here? How did you get in?"

"Mr Sheridan..." began William.

"Mr Sheridan what?" demanded Mrs Barr and flung open the door to reveal Mr Sheridan in his wheelchair with Tilly standing beside him. Mr Barr pushed William into the room beside them.

"So you thought you'd come and rob an old man, did you?" said Mrs Barr. "When we weren't here to protect him. Some kids start young in crime. You read about it in the paper but you don't expect them to be living on your doorstep."

"Where did you break in?" barked Mr Barr.

"Mr Sheridan invited us in," retorted Tilly.

"Tell me another one!"

"That is perfectly true," said Mr Sheridan.

"You couldn't go down and open the door for them."

"Young William here climbed the drainpipe. Very agile he was too."

"I'd call that breaking and entering. I think we might have to call the police."

"It's not breaking in if you're invited," William pointed out.

"Who's going to believe him?" said Mrs Barr, meaning Mr Sheridan. "His head's muddled half the time."

"No, it is not!" Tilly's eyes sparked with anger. "His head is perfectly fine if other people don't try to muddle it."

"So what brought you round here in the first place?" asked Mr Barr.

"We came to tell Mr Sheridan that you were trying to cheat him."

"Is that right, little girl?" Mr Barr let go of William and came over to Tilly. "What makes you say a silly thing like that?"

"You want to sell his land for a golf course without him knowing. That's a crime if you ask me."

"I don't think I want to ask you anything," Mr Barr said softly.

Tilly was trembling. She could see, now that she was close up to him, what a horrible man he was. He had mean-looking eyes.

"She's got a point, though, Mr Barr," put in Mr Sheridan. "You remember that paper you asked me to sign?"

"Just you stay out of this, Mr Sheridan. Don't bother your head with it. We'll deal with it." To his wife Mr Barr said, "Why don't you take Mr Sheridan along to his room for a little nap, dear? He might even like a sleeping pill."

"Nap? I don't need a nap," protested Mr Sheridan, but Mrs Barr had already taken hold of the handles of his chair.

"No, he doesn't need a nap." William moved to block their path to the door.

"Looking for trouble, are you?" asked Mr Barr, his voice becoming even more threatening. "You might get more than you bargained for."

"Why don't you call the police?" said Tilly. "And then you can charge us with breaking in and robbing."

"I think we might be able to deal with this ourselves. Take Mr Sheridan to his room, dear," he said again to his wife.

"No!" shouted Tilly and William together.

"Nobody says no to me," said Mr Barr. "Now the best thing would be for the two of you to say you're sorry and tell Mr Sheridan that it was nothing but a pack of lies you were telling him. Then you can go home and we can forget all about it. And he will too. You were imagining things, weren't you, Mr Sheridan?"

He broke off, frowning, as a car was heard on the gravel outside.

"It'll be my mum," cried Tilly. "She

might have got a lift with William's mum. I rang her, you see. On the mobile." She pulled the phone from her pocket and held it above her head.

"Tilly!" yelled her mum down below.

Tilly ran over to the window and waved. She had been right: William's mother was there, too. They had come in her car.

"Right then, you two," ordered Mr Barr. "We'll take you downstairs to your mothers."

He and his wife bustled them out of the room, not even giving them time to say goodbye to Mr Sheridan. They were frog-marched down the stairs and Mr Barr opened the door to reveal the two mothers on the doorstep.

"Are you all right, Tilly? William?" they chorused.

"They're fine," said Mrs Barr in a tinkly voice, not at all like the one she'd been using upstairs. "They've just been having a little adventure. But we know what children are like so we're prepared to say no more about it."

"What have you been up to?" asked William's mother.

"He climbed up the drainpipe and came into the house while we were out," Mr Barr replied before William could speak. "Boys will be boys, I suppose!"

"William!" cried his mother, horrified. "You climbed up the drainpipe?"

"They're making it sound all wrong." Tilly was feeling desperate. "They were trying to steal from Mr Sheridan."

"What nonsense!" tinkled Mrs Barr.

"We must call the police," urged Tilly.

"Oh, I did," said her mother. "You sounded as if something really serious was going on so I rang them. Is that not them now?"

Two policemen were arriving at

that moment in a squad car. Mr Barr went forward to meet them.

"Sorry you've been troubled, officers. There's been a little misunderstanding but it's all been sorted out now."

CHAPTER 9

"No," cried Tilly, racing over to them, "it's not at all sorted out. You must come upstairs and speak to Mr Sheridan."

"There would be no point in that," Mr Barr butted in. "Mr Sheridan's memory is not reliable. It's inclined to wander a bit."

"Not that much," snapped Tilly. "They just say it does."

"Well, I don't know." The

policemen frowned. "Maybe we should have a word with Mr Sheridan. We'd like to know just what has been going on here."

The Barrs could not refuse. They all trooped up the stairs, the two children, their mothers, the Barrs, and the two policemen. Mr Sheridan looked astonished when they all came into his room.

"Sorry about this intrusion, sir,"

said the policeman who seemed to be the spokesman. "But we'd like to ask you one or two questions, if you don't mind."

"This boy here," Mr Barr waved at William, "William Beattie, climbed up the drainpipe while we were out, officer. He admits it."

"Is this true, William?" asked the constable.

William nodded.

"I invited him," put in Mr Sheridan.

"Now, Mr Sheridan," began Mrs Barr, but she was stopped by the police. She turned to them. "He imagines things at times. I should know. I look after him."

"Please, Mrs Barr, we wish to question Mr Sheridan all the same."

"The children think that Mr Barr got me to sell my land for a golf course," said Mr Sheridan.

"And you haven't?"

"I certainly don't wish to."

"I see."

"Like I told you, officer," Mrs Barr tried to interrupt again, once more, without success. The police ignored her.

"Have you signed anything, Mr Sheridan?" they asked.

"I do sign things from time to time."

"We'll obviously have to look into this."

"Officer, you are getting hold of the wrong end of the stick." Mr Barr spoke in a voice that showed he was determined to be heard. "Mr Sheridan said he wanted to sell the land. I brought a lawyer to see him, we discussed it, and he signed of his own free will. It was witnessed by a lawyer. The document can be produced."

"A crooked one, I bet," muttered Tilly.

"Shush, Tilly," chided her mother.

"You've forgotten all that, haven't you, Mr Sheridan?" Mrs Barr was back to the tinkly voice. "Don't worry

117

your head about it, dear."

"If he has signed voluntarily," said the policeman, "and it was all legal and above board, then there's nothing we can do."

"Exactly." Mr Barr nodded, as if that was it settled. "My wife and I do not intend to press charges against the children for breaking and entering. We will overlook it, on this occasion. But not if it were to happen again."

"We didn't break and enter!" said William. "That's a lie!"

"Shush, William." His mother frowned at him.

"There's something else," added Tilly. "Mr Sheridan told us there was a break-in and all his silver was stolen. Did you know that?"

The policeman frowned. "I don't recall that being reported. Do you, Ian?"

His colleague shook his head. "I would certainly remember if it had been. We'd have been along to investigate. Why did you think your silver was stolen, Mr Sheridan?"

"Mr Barr said so."

"Was there a burglary, Mr Barr?"

"It's just his imagination running riot again."

"If there was no burglary, where then is the silver?" asked the policeman.

"It should be in the dining room," said Mr Sheridan.

Mr Barr looked at Mrs Barr.

"Perhaps you'd better take us to the dining room," suggested the policeman, "and show us where the silver is kept."

"Well, as a matter of fact," said Mr Barr, clearing his throat, "there was a robbery. This is a little awkward." He took a break to cough. "We've been meaning to report it, but it only happened two days ago and we haven't had time. We thought, too, that it might have been mislaid somehow."

"It was last month that it was stolen," declared Mr Sheridan. "I definitely remember. It was the day of my birthday and I said, "Oh dear, that's not a very nice birthday present!" I was ninety-two!"

"You don't look as old as that, Mr Sheridan," said Tilly.

"Thank you, Tilly." He inclined his head, acknowledging her compliment.

"I think," said the policeman, "that we'll all go along to the station and take some statements. Not you, of course, Mr Sheridan. I'll radio for someone to come along and take yours here.

CHAPTER 10

At the police station in town the Barrs
told their side of the story and Tilly
and William told theirs. Their mothers
had accompanied them.

"We'll be in touch," the desk
sergeant informed them, once he'd
taken their statements. "I would ask
that none of you leave the area in case
we need to question you further."

"We've no intention of leaving the
area." Mrs Barr was indignant. "Why

should we do that? Since we're innocent. And we have Mr Sheridan to look after. We would never leave him in the lurch."

"Mr Sheridan might not want them to look after him," Tilly addressed the sergeant. "Now that he knows they've been stealing from him."

"She can't be allowed to get away with saying this." Mr Barr glared at her. "She's blackening our name."

"He's right," the sergeant told Tilly. "You must watch what you say. We haven't charged anyone with anything."

The Barrs left before Tilly and William and their mothers.

"They'll work on Mr Sheridan," said William gloomily. "They'll get him to change what he said. I know they will!"

"Leave it, William." His mum

put her hand on his arm.

"Are you not going to do anything?"
Tilly asked the
sergeant. "William's
right. They'll get
Mr Sheridan all
mixed up so that
he won't know
whether he's coming
or going. They might
even drug him!"

"I told you – you've got to be
careful what you say!"

"We're going home now, Tilly," said
her mum. "You must understand,
officer, that they're very worked up
about the old man."

"I know, I appreciate that. But we
can't do anything without proof."

"How will you get it?" demanded
Tilly.

"We'll put a tracer on the silver

round the antique shops."

They had to be content with that. When they got home they felt uneasy about Mr Sheridan and kept wondering how he was getting on. Tilly's mother rang the minister and asked if he would look in at Sheridan Hall. He did but when he asked after Mr Sheridan he was told he was sleeping. Tilly woke up a few times in the night thinking about Mr Sheridan being all alone in the big house with Mr and Mrs Barr.

William came in after breakfast and they hung about in the garden, watching the road in case the police came back. Their mothers had told them that they were to stay put and not even to think about wandering off anywhere.

"We don't want any more goings on like yesterday's." Tilly's mother had been firm and Tilly knew there was no point in arguing. "I almost had a heart attack when I got your phone call."

Just before lunchtime, they saw two police cars going past, with two policemen in each car. Fifteen to twenty minutes later the cars came back. This time a policeman was sitting in the back of each car, with Mr Barr beside one of them, and Mrs Barr the other. Neither of them looked over to where Tilly and William were standing.

"Maybe they've been arrested," cried Tilly excitedly. They hadn't been able to make out if the Barrs were handcuffed or not.

"They might just have been taken in for questioning again," Tilly's mother warned them when they told her.

"Couldn't you ring the police station and find out?" asked Tilly.

"No, I could not. They'll not want me annoying them. If they have anything to tell us they'll phone or else call."

They were on tenterhooks all afternoon. It seemed a long day. They started a game of Monopoly but couldn't seem to concentrate.

Then, around four o'clock, one of the policemen they'd met yesterday arrived. They ran out to meet him as he was getting out of his car.

"The Barrs have been arrested," he told them, "and charged with the theft of Mr Sheridan's silver and a number of other items as well."

"Hurrah!" cried Tilly.

"We located them at a shop in Edinburgh and the owner was able to identify Mr Barr as the seller. It seems the Barrs have been at it for years, plundering all the valuables in the house and selling them off."

"What about the land they sold for the golf course?" asked William.

"We'll be investigating the lawyer who co-signed the deed of sale of Mr Sheridan's land."

"What about Mr Sheridan?" asked Tilly. "Who's going to be looking after him now? He can't stay there on his own."

"We've called the Social Services in and they're along there now. They'll make arrangements for him."

"I hope they don't put him in a home," said Tilly.

In the morning, their mothers allowed them to walk along to call at the house. A social worker opened the door and was friendly enough but she didn't ask them in. They were terribly busy sorting things out but they'd been fortunate to get hold of a very nice

couple who were free and good at looking after elderly people. They were called Mr and Mrs Young.

"He'll be in excellent hands, I can assure you of that. So you won't have to worry about him now."

"Will you tell him we called?" asked Tilly.

"Of course."

"Just say Tilly and William were asking for him."

"I'll certainly do that."

When Tilly got home she told her

mum about Mr Sheridan's new housekeepers.

"That's him more or less settled then," said her mum.

"But we're not, are we?" said Tilly.

CHAPTER 11

There had still been no response to Tilly's postcard in the village shop. Her mum was beginning to think they'd have to move into town. She'd been offered a flat above a shop to rent at a reasonable rate.

"But I don't want to live there!" protested Tilly. "And don't start telling me about beggars!"

"I don't know why you didn't put your painting in for the competition."

Tilly had shown it to her. "It was very good."

"I didn't want to."

"Why not?"

"Just because." Tilly had other plans for it though she hadn't said anything about that to either her mother or William. She was just about to go and call for him.

They had been asked to tea with Mr Sheridan that afternoon. Mrs Young had phoned to invite them, and she had sounded nice. "He's very much looking forward to seeing the two of you. He's talked about you so much!"

Tilly put her painting in a folder and went next door.

"What have you got there?" asked William, eyeing the folder under her arm.

"Not telling."

"Don't then!"

When they were walking along the road she told William about the flat in town. "I'd have to go to a new school. I'd hate that."

"It'd be a lot quieter in ours, though."

She reached out to biff him but he ducked.

"I've told you before, Tilly. Just refuse to go."

"A big deal that would be."

"If the Ewe was to get the sheriff in to remove you it'd make an awful stink in the village. She wouldn't like that. You might get your picture in the *Gazette*." The *Gazette* was the local paper.

They turned in at the drive. Mr Young was hacking away at the undergrowth under the rhododendron trees. Mr Barr had never bothered to keep the drive tidy.

Mr Young stopped work to greet them. "So you're the two heroes who rescued Mr Sheridan!" He had red cheeks and twinkly eyes. They liked him on sight. "You'd better go on up. He can't wait for you coming."

They went to the back door. Mrs Young opened it and straightaway took them upstairs to Mr Sheridan's sitting room. She had made lemon meringue pie, iced biscuits with cherries on top and a chocolate cake for them coming. The food was all set out on the table.

Mr Sheridan came forward in his wheelchair to meet them. He shook hands with each in turn and said how much he had looked forward to their visit.

"I'm sure all children like chocolate cake." He couldn't stop beaming at them. "So I asked Mrs Young to make one. As a little reward for helping me. You see, I like chocolate cake too!"

"We didn't do an awful lot," said William.

"Oh, but you did! You did a great deal and I am extremely grateful. You saved me from Mr and Mrs Barr. They always seemed to be good at managing things but I never did like them very much, I have to confess. But I had no idea they were quite as wicked as that."

was asked to pour the tea from a white china teapot decorated with pink roses. It looked old, and valuable. She took great care not to spill a single drop of the tea on the white lace cloth. Her mum would have been proud of her, and amazed. She often complained that Tilly was sloppy and spilt things. But Tilly was not being sloppy that afternoon.

"I had good news this morning," announced Mr Sheridan. "The matter of my land has been cleared up. I am so relieved."

"So are we," said Tilly.

"The document that I'd signed was declared illegal. They couldn't trace the lawyer. He'd vanished. Or he'd never existed, not as a lawyer anyway."

"So the hills belong to you again," said William.

"They do."

"You won't be selling them for a golf course?" asked Tilly.

"Certainly not. I loved seeing the goats as a boy. My eyes are no longer good enough to see them, even with my glasses." His glasses had been mended and he was wearing them now. "They never come very close to the house, sadly for me."

Tilly lifted her folder and took out her picture. "I would like to give you this, Mr Sheridan." She handed it to him.

He took her picture in his hands.

He smiled. "It's the goats! How wonderful. I shall have it framed and put on the wall so that I will always be able to see them. Thank you, Tilly, for such a lovely present."

"I'm glad you like it."

"Oh, I certainly do. That reminds me, Mrs Young heard in the village that you and your mother were going to have to leave your house. Is that true?"

"The Ewe – I mean Mrs Ewbank – needs it for her nephew."

"In that case, I was wondering if you would like to come and live in my gate-house?"

"Live in your gate-house?"

"Well, it's empty now that the Barrs have left. They used to live there but Mr and Mrs Young are staying in the house with me so they don't need it. It's nice for me to have the company."

"Do you actually mean it?" cried Tilly. "Really and truly? Live in the gate-house? My mum and me?"

"Of course I mean it. Yes, really and truly. I mean everything I say."

Tilly ran over to the wheelchair and gave Mr Sheridan a hug.

"It's a long time since anyone has done that to me." His eyes were shining behind their glasses.

"You can be a kind of grandpa to me if you like," she offered. "Since I don't have one. I've sort of adopted all William's aunts and uncles."

"I would like that very much indeed, Tilly," said Mr Sheridan gravely.

At the end of the week, William heard that he had won first prize in the painting competition.

"That's 'cause I didn't put mine in," said Tilly and he stuck out his tongue at her. She laughed and thumped him on the back. "That was brill, William! I knew you'd win."

The prize was a pair of binoculars. William was thrilled. Now he could go bird-watching.

"And we'll be able to get a better look at the goats with them," added Tilly.

"We can? Who says I'll let you have a shot?"

She made a face at him and he danced away from her, waving the binoculars aloft.

Two days later, Tilly and her mum moved into the gate-house of Sheridan Hall. They loved the little house and Mr Sheridan signed a lease, of his own free will, giving them the right to live there for as long as they wanted.

"Even after I'm gone."

"You won't go for a long time," predicted Tilly.

"If you say so, Tilly." Mr Sheridan smiled and looked up at her picture of the goats on his wall.